Sheriff Sally Gopher

AND THE

THANKSGIVING CAPER

story and pictures by
Robert Quackenbush

Lothrop, Lee & Shepard Books
New York

For my son, Piet,
and for my nephew, John

Library of Congress Cataloging in Publication Data
Quackenbush, Robert M.   Sheriff Sally Gopher and the Thanksgiving caper.
Summary: An election is held at Pebble Junction to see whether a turkey, a vulture, or a
duck should reign as the Thanksgiving symbol.   [1. Thanksgiving Day—Fiction.
2. Animals—Fiction] I. Title. PZ7.Q16Sj   [E]   82-135
ISBN 0-688-01292-2   AACR2   ISBN 0-688-01293-0 (lib. bdg.)

Virgil Vulture stormed into Sheriff Sally Gopher's office.

"I protest!" he cried. "The statue of Terence Turkey in the square is a fake! Halt the work!"

Virgil Vulture's objections were so loud that the sheriff's dozing deputies, Summers and Winters Jack Rabbit, Rosa Roadrunner, and Gracie Gecko, fell out of their chairs.

"What do you mean, Virgil?" said Sheriff Sally, looking out the window that faced the town square. "It looks like ole Terence Turkey to me, and he's always been the model for Pebble Junction's Thanksgiving corn feast. After all, it was his ancestor, Miles Turkey, who graced the table at the first Thanksgiving and who became a national symbol. So the statue *should* look like Terence."

"That's just it!" cried Virgil. "Why does Terence get all the honors? My ancestor Jonathan Vulture was also at the Pilgrims' first Thanksgiving."

"*He was?*" cried Sheriff Sally Gopher and her astonished deputies.

"Of course he was," snapped Virgil. "Everyone knows what valuable scavengers we vultures are. Who do you think cleaned up the mess after the feast?"

"Ugh, disgusting," said the Jack Rabbit twins.

"Quiet, deputies," said Sheriff Sally. "Virgil has a right to be heard. Let's see the mayor about this, Virgil," she went on, following the vulture outside. "I'd like to know what *he* says."

Virgil went over to the post where Jake Horse was hitched.

"Mayor," said Virgil, "the sheriff said I should see you about my complaint."

"Just a minute," said Jake, who was Pebble Junction's mayor as well as Sheriff Sally's horse. He was also—depending on the hat he was wearing—the clerk, chief cook, and bottle washer for the only hotel in town.

Jake reached for a stovepipe hat that was attached to his saddle, and placed it on his head. "Now, Virgil, state your business," he said.

Virgil told the mayor about his objections to the town's Thanksgiving Day plans. A crowd began to gather as he talked. Terence Turkey was there, as well as Sid Snake, Dirk Duck, and quite a few of Pebble Junction's other leading citizens.

"Hmmm, hmmm, hmmm," said Jake when Virgil was through. "This *is* a problem. What can we do about it?"

"What about voting?" someone asked.

"A good idea," said the mayor. "We shall have an election to choose who is to be the symbol for our Thanksgiving Day festivities—Virgil or Terence. And you can be in charge of it, Sheriff. I must save my strength for the big corn feast. I plan to stuff myself that day."

Just then Dirk Duck spoke up. "Wait a durn minute, Mayor. I have something to say, too. My ancestors also played a role in that first Thanksgiving."

At this, a murmur rose from the crowd.

"Settle down, everyone," said Jake with a sigh. When all was quiet again, the mayor asked Dirk Duck to tell his story.

"It all started in Holland," began Dirk Duck, "where my ancestors lived. Many of the Pilgrims who fled England lived in Leiden, Holland, before they sailed to America. In Holland they learned many new customs, including the October third 'hutspot' feast.

"The first hutspot feast was in 1574, when the Dutch drove Spanish troops out of Leiden. They did this by opening the dikes and flooding approaches to the city so ships could come and save them. When the Spanish troops heard about the relief ships, they fled, leaving behind a hodge-podge of meat, potatoes, carrots, and onions—called 'hutspot'—still simmering in Spanish pots. The hungry citizens of Leiden ate the meal with thanks and prepared a hutspot feast every year thereafter."

"Interesting, Dirk," said the mayor. "But what does that tradition have to do with the Pilgrims' first Thanksgiving?"

"Everything," answered Dirk. "Some scholars believe that the Pilgrims who settled in America adapted the custom to be their own day of thanks for having found freedom in a new land, for having survived a long, cruel winter, and for having grown enough food to last them through another winter season.

"So, you see," Dirk Duck finished, "*my* Dutch ancestors should also be honored at our Thanksgiving celebration. And I would be happy to model for the statue you place in the square."

"So now we have *three* wanting to enter the race," said Jake. "Anyone else?"

The crowd was silent.

"Very well," said the mayor. "Campaigning shall begin at once, and the election will be held in the square one week from today. That will give us one week to put up the proper decorations in time for Thanksgiving. Voting will be ancient Greek style, using colored stones instead of paper ballots. A brown stone will represent Terence, a white stone will represent Dirk, and a black stone will represent Virgil. Whoever gets the most stones cast for him will be the symbol for our holiday. And may the best bird win!"

"Hooray!" shouted the crowd.

With that, Jake Horse removed his mayor's hat—calling the meeting to an end—and everyone ran to get ready for the election. The corn statue of Terence was taken down, and election posters and banners were placed around the town.

Sheriff Sally Gopher maintained order during the campaign. She assigned posts to each of her deputies, who were to report anything that might keep the election from being a fair and honest one.

"I promise to make this coming Thanksgiving Day one that you will never forget," cried Virgil Vulture in his campaign speech. "Vote for me."

"I promise to carry on the traditions of the first Thanksgiving as they were learned from my Dutch ancestors," vowed Dirk Duck from the opposite side of the street. "Vote for me."

A few paces away Terence Turkey proclaimed, "I promise to carry on as the true symbol of Thanksgiving Day. Vote for me!"

Campaign week passed quickly, and soon election day arrived. The voting booth was set up in the square. One at a time, the voters entered the booth and dropped their secret stones into the ballot box.

That afternoon, Summers Jack Rabbit burst into Sheriff Sally's office and said, "The first box of stones was just counted, Sheriff. Terence is in the lead. It looks like the turkey symbol may stay."

Just then, Virgil Vulture passed by the open door and overheard the deputy's report. "Don't be so sure," he said from the doorway. "Don't be so sure." Turning abruptly, he stomped off again.

"Let's keep an eye on him, Summers," said Sheriff Sally.

The sheriff and her deputy followed Virgil to the square. The vulture was the last to vote. He entered the booth with a little paper sack, like the ones other voters had carried to hide their stones.

After Virgil had voted, the judges emptied the ballot box for the second and last time. To their surprise, all the stones were black. They counted them and wrote the final results on the tally board. Virgil had won!

The crowd went wild. Some citizens were happy, some were sad, and some shouted, "Recount! Recount!" Things were getting out of hand, so Sheriff Sally stepped forward.

"Listen, everyone!" she cried. "We are losing valuable time from our Thanksgiving preparations. Virgil has won. Arguing about it might delay our feast day. It's just a symbol that has been changed—not our whole wonderful holiday. Can't we bring this election to a close?"

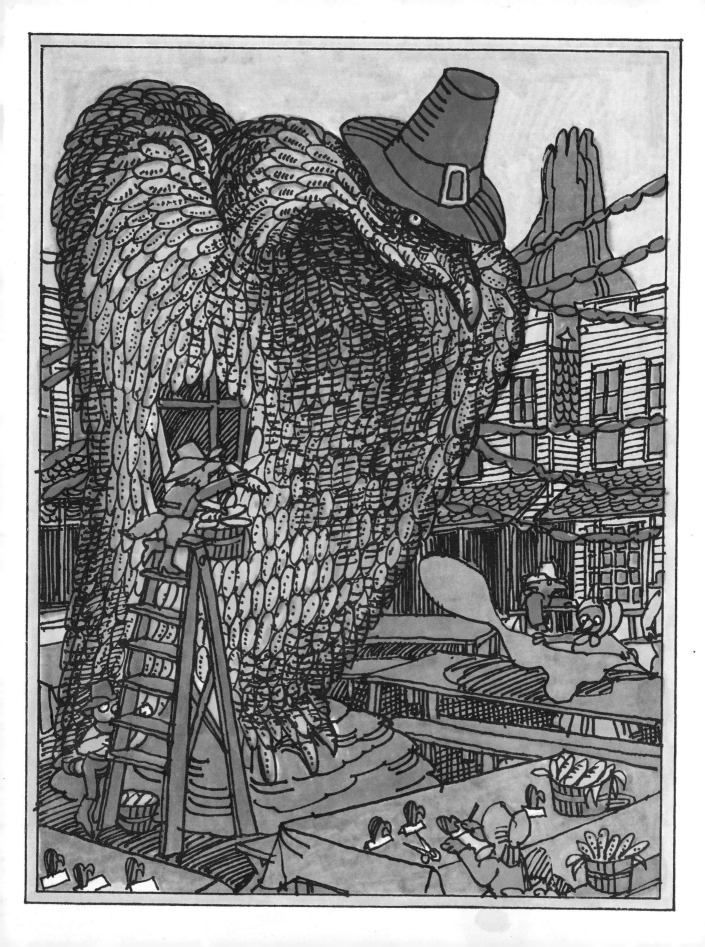

There were nods and cheers, and soon everyone agreed that Sally was right and that Virgil was the rightful winner. Then the townspeople set to work redoing their Thanksgiving decorations. The statue in the square was made to look like Virgil, and so were all the favors. As the days went by, though, it became clear that something was wrong.

"What gloom seems to have settled over this town!" Gracie Gecko blurted out one afternoon.

"The decorations don't help," said Summers Jack Rabbit. "It seems strange to have a vulture for our Thanksgiving symbol."

"That's for sure," agreed Winters Jack Rabbit.

"Quiet, deputies," said Sheriff Sally. "You'll just upset folks with your complaints."

It was too late. Mother Quail had heard them talking.

"Your deputies are right, Sheriff," she said. "There *is* gloom cast over what should be a happy time for everyone. Can't Virgil be stopped? I hear that he is even changing the menu from Indian corn recipes to things only *he* likes."

Just then a small black object whizzed past Sheriff Sally's foot and landed in a puddle. It was a quail chick's marble, and Sheriff Sally went to rescue it. But when she picked it out of the water, it was no longer black. It was brown!

"That's strange, chicks," said Sheriff Sally. "Where did you get this marble? It appears to have been painted."

"It's one of the stones from the election," explained a chick. "The judges gave them to us so we could play marbles. See, they are all like that one."

"You don't say," said Sheriff Sally. "Let me borrow a few of them. I'll return them to you in a jiffy."

Sheriff Sally took her deputies aside.

"Someone colored these stones so that the election would come out in Virgil's favor," she said. "But who?"

"What about Virgil himself?" said Summers Jack Rabbit. "He was the last to vote. He could have poured a bottle of quick-drying ink into the ballot box."

"Of course!" cried Sheriff Sally. "Let's go talk to him."

They all ran to Virgil's house. In the trash can in his yard they found the paper sack he had carried into the voting booth. Inside the bag was an empty bottle of black ink!

"Nice try, Virgil," said Sheriff Sally, holding up the evidence. "But cheaters never win. It's a good thing for you that it wasn't a regular election, or I would have to haul you in and lock you up. I have a good mind to, anyway, and throw away the key."

"Please don't do that to me," Virgil begged. "I made a mistake. I don't really want to be the feast symbol. We vultures are loners. We hate huge gatherings. Give the job to Terence. He really should have won."

"I'm glad you feel that way, Virgil," said Sheriff Sally. "And I've changed my mind about you. You *would* be a good symbol for a holiday, but not this one. How about National Clean-Up Day? I'll propose it to the mayor."

For once, Virgil was speechless. So the sheriff and her deputies went back to town. They announced that Virgil had resigned and that Terence was their holiday symbol once more. By now, everyone was so glad to have tradition restored that no one objected—not even Dirk Duck.

With only two days left till Thanksgiving, the townspeople worked at fever pitch to set everything right again.

By the time the big day rolled around, the election was forgotten and Virgil was forgiven. He was the only one to stay home, waiting, as he always did, for his fun to begin at clean-up time.

So, in the end, Pebble Junction's holiday was a perfect success. It was so perfect that everyone vowed to keep to tradition at future Thanksgivings. And they stuck to their word.

Robert Quackenbush has illustrated over one hundred books, nearly half of which he has also written. His works include picture books, song books, fiction, nonfiction, and easy readers, such as his well-loved Detective Mole series. His books have received awards and citations from AIGA and the Society of Illustrators, and his graphics have been exhibited in leading museums in this country. Mr. Quackenbush lives in New York City with his wife, Margery, a fashion designer and teacher, and their son, Piet.